A Day at the Sugar Bush
Making Maple Syrup

Text by Megan Faulkner   Photographs by Wally Randall

Scholastic Canada Ltd.
Toronto New York London Auckland Sydney
Mexico City New Delhi Hong Kong Buenos Aires

For my grandfather, whose enthusiasm for learning is a constant inspiration.
— M.F.

For my parents, Warren and Pat Randall,
who always encouraged my love of the outdoors and photography.
— W.R.

Cover and interior photographs by Wally Randall, with the following exceptions:
Page 23 (lower left): Adam Krawesky
Page 26 (lower left): Sandy Flat Sugar Bush, Warkworth, Ontario
Page 28: Edward Scrope Shrapnel, *Maple Sugar Making*, image located in *Upper Canada Sketches*, facing page 78, 2000 85 9376,
National Archives of Canada, 030930-0953
Page 29 (left): Sandy Flat Sugar Bush, Warkworth, Ontario; (right): Adam Krawesky

National Library of Canada Cataloguing in Publication

Faulkner, Megan
A day at the sugarbush : making maple syrup / Megan Faulkner, Wally Randall.

ISBN 0-7791-1411-6

1. Sugar maple—Tapping—Juvenile literature. 2. Maple syrup—Juvenile literature. I. Randall, Wally II. Title.

SB239.M3F38 2004   j633.6'45   C2003-904904-3

ISBN 10 0-7791-1411-6 / ISBN 13 978-0-7791-1411-5

6 5 4 3 2   Printed and bound in Singapore   09 10 11 12

It's the first week of spring. The days are warm and the nights are cold. It's time to visit the sugar bush!

We'll find out how tree sap is made into maple syrup and maple sugar.

3

There are many kinds of maple tree. In the sugar bush, the most common kind is the sugar maple, because it has the sweetest sap.

Sap is the liquid that flows inside the tree. It carries nutrients to the leaves, branches, trunk and roots.

During sugaring-off season, when a hole is drilled into the trunk of a maple tree, the clear, watery sap begins to flow out.

A spout called a spile is hammered into the hole. The sap drips into a pail that hangs from the spile.

We taste the fresh sap
from the maple tree. It is
slightly sweet.

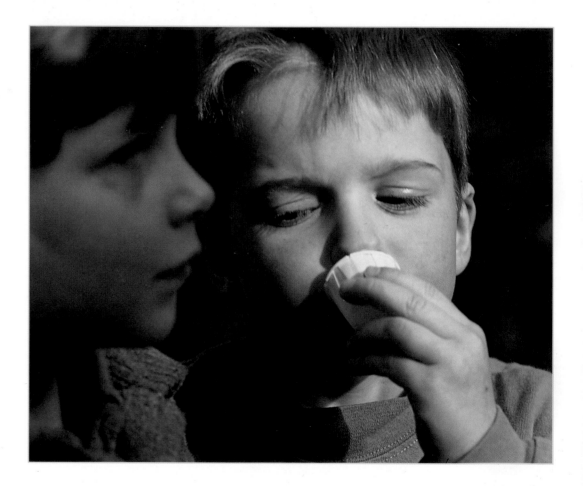

Then we taste some sap
that has been boiled into
maple syrup. It is *very*
sweet.

We see how pioneers emptied the sap buckets into bigger pails, and carried them with a yoke to the sugar kettles.

We try it, too.

An easier way to collect the sap was to pour it into a gathering tank that horses could pull.

Once the sap is collected, it must be boiled for a long time. The water in the sap turns into steam. This is called evaporation.

Nowadays, many maple syrup producers use plastic tubes to carry the sap from the trees to a stainless-steel holding tank.

Sometimes a vacuum pump sucks the sap through the tubes.

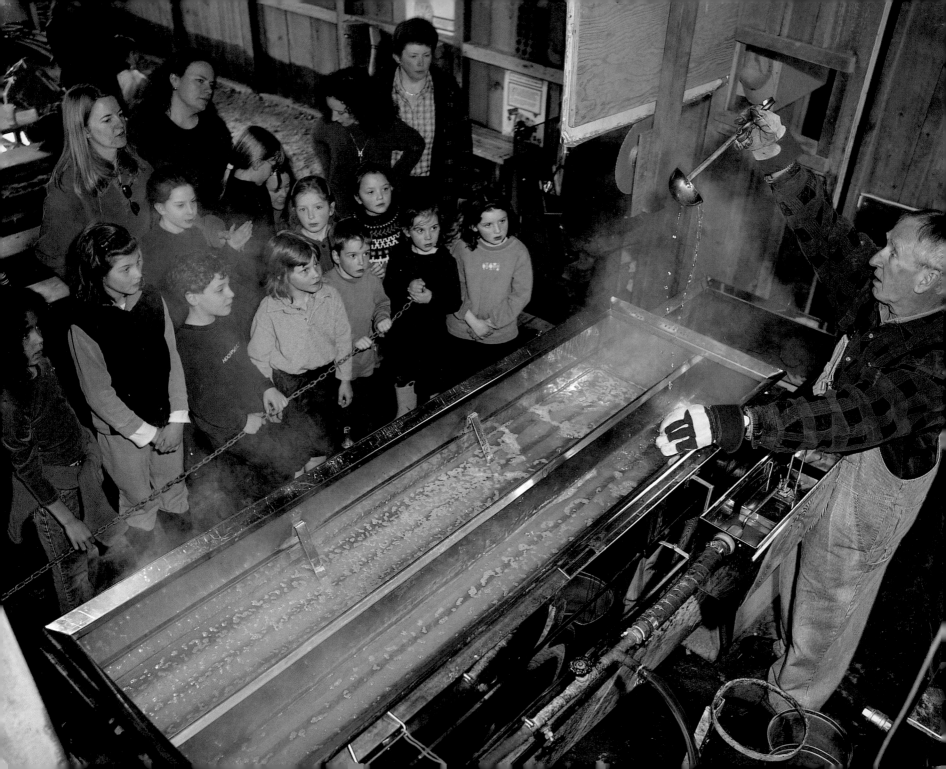

We watch the sap boil in the compartments of a large, flat-bottomed pan called an evaporator.

We add more wood to the fire to keep the sap boiling. It gets thicker and thicker.

Finally, the sap moves to the last compartment, called the finishing pan.

The last traces of excess water evaporate, leaving behind sweet, golden-brown maple syrup. A tap is opened to drain the finished syrup.

It is filtered twice to remove any dirt.

To do this, the pioneers strained it through cheesecloth.

The hot syrup is poured
into bottles and sealed.
Now it is ready to enjoy!

To make maple candy,
the syrup is boiled
longer. We watch it
become very thick.

Then it is poured into
moulds where it hardens.

If the syrup is boiled until all the moisture is gone, it becomes maple sugar. Early Canadian cooks depended on maple sugar to add a sweet flavour to their cooking and baking.

Before we leave the sugar bush,
there's a special treat for us.
Pancakes with maple syrup.
Delicious!

The First Taste of Maple

E.S.Shrapnel

Long ago, before Europeans arrived in Canada, Native peoples in the eastern woodlands were tapping maple trees and using the sap to make maple syrup and sugar. How was the sweet sap discovered? An Iroquois legend tells that a boy noticed a squirrel bite off a sugar maple twig and lick the sap that oozed out. When he tasted the sap himself, he found that it was sweet.

To collect the sap, Native peoples made V-shaped gashes in the trunks of sugar maples and inserted curved pieces of wood or bark. These were the first spiles. The sap dripped into birchbark buckets, hollowed-out logs, or clay pots.

For several nights they left the containers of sap to freeze, and removed the ice. This meant the water content was reduced in the sap that was left. Then, over and over, they heated stones in the coals of a fire and placed them in the containers to steam off the remaining water. Hardened into cakes, the maple sugar kept well, sometimes in wooden moulds or birchbark containers.

Early settlers arriving in the eastern woodlands learned the sugaring-off process from the Native peoples. To reach the sap inside the trees, they drilled small holes and pushed in hollowed stems. Sometimes horse-drawn sleighs were used to pull the pails of sap back to the sugar camp. There, large cast-iron cauldrons were suspended over the fire to boil the liquid down.

Today maple syrup is produced in large quantities, using evaporators, plastic tubes and vacuum pumps. But the basic process of tapping maple trees and boiling off the water remains the same. Canadians are proud to supply eighty-five percent of the world's maple syrup. Ninety percent of that comes from the province of Quebec.

Tire Sur Neige

Native maple syrup makers were quick to discover the delicious combination of hot maple syrup and fresh, cold snow. Today in the sugar bush, especially in Quebec, it is a time-honoured tradition to pour a stream of hot syrup onto clean snow and roll it onto a stick, for a warm, chewy mouthful of maple taffy.

Syrup on Snow Sundae

You can make your own version of *tire sur neige* at home. Simply pour pure maple syrup over a scoop or two of snowy-white vanilla ice cream. Top with maple candy, whole or crumbled. Mmm, cold and sweet!

Notes

Page 2: Canadian maple syrup is graded as Canada #1, #2 or #3. There are five colour classes — extra light, light, medium, amber and dark. The light has the most delicate maple flavour, and the dark has the strongest maple flavour.

Page 5: Besides the sugar maple, syrup can be made from the red maple, the silver maple and the black maple, but the sap must be boiled for a much longer time, and produces a darker syrup with a slightly different taste.

Page 7: The circumference of a tree must measure 80 centimetres at chest height before it can be tapped. When it grows to 120 centimetres, sap can be withdrawn from two tap holes. If it reaches 160 centimetres, three tap holes can be used. Only very large trees of 200 centimetres in circumference can support four tap holes.

Page 14-15: On a slope, gravity can carry the sap through the plastic tubes to the holding tank. On level ground, however, a vacuum pump is used to draw the sap through a vast network of tubing.

Page 19: Forty pails of sap must be collected, and boiled for many hours, in order to produce one pail of maple syrup.

Page 20: Today, modern evaporator equipment includes specialized sap filters to remove impurities.

Page 23: Maple candy can be clear or opaque. Depending on how much it is heated, how rapidly it is cooled, and whether or not it is stirred, it can take many different forms. All are delicious.

Acknowledgements

Special thanks to the children of the Toronto Waldorf School who accompanied us on our visit to the sugar bush, for their interest and enthusiasm.

Thanks also to the Kortright Centre for Conservation and to Bruce's Mill Conservation Area for sharing their maple syrup festivals with us, and for the generous help provided by their knowledgeable staffs.

The author wishes to thank Dr. David Fayle for his expert advice, Adam Krawesky for lending his talent at the last minute, and Heather Patterson for her invaluable contributions.